CHINESE MYTHOLOGY

CLAUDE HELFT

CHINESE MYTHOLOGY

Stories of Creation and Invention

Illustrations by
CHEN JIANG HONG

Translated from the French
by Michael Hariton and Claudia Bedrick

ENCHANTED LION BOOKS
New York

For Flo, Guillaume and Alice

For Marin 安虎
(Chinese name: Peaceful Tiger)

and Xiao-Lin 晓琳

For François 星座
(Constellation, in Chinese)

For Alfred

Artistic Direction and Graphic Conception:
Isabelle Gibert

Layout: Maud Cornu

Story Consultant and Pronunciation
Guide for American Edition:
Hsinyi Peng

First American Edition published in 2007 by
Enchanted Lion Books
45 Main Street, Suite 519
Brooklyn, NY 11201

Originally published in French as
La Mythologie Chinoise
Text and Illustrations © 2002 by Actes Sud

Translation © 2007 by Enchanted Lion Books

[A CIP record is on file with the Library of Congress]

ISBN-13: 978-1-59270-074-5
ISBN-10: 1-59270-074-8

Printed in China

2 4 6 8 10 9 7 5 3 1

CONTENTS

1

THE THREE SOVEREIGNS

How was the universe born? For the Chinese, in mystery.

In those vast lands that only later came to be called China, they tell many stories about how the world was made.

Since ancient times, people have wanted to know what astute god or architect set up the world for all eternity in such a way that humans have simply seen it continue while giving thanks to the gods for creating all that is. The oldest of these stories stretches back to a time when heaven and earth were inhabited by mythical creatures, and dragons and gods moved about in raging seas and numinous heavens. This was a time before humans existed.

THE GIANT'S FOOTPRINT

In a paradise of the immortals, Hua-xu, a beautiful goddess, bathed in the fresh water of Thunder Lake. As she stepped out of the water, an extraordinary footprint caught her eye. It was the outline of a foot so huge that only a giant could have made it. Could it belong to the owner of the place, the god of thunder himself, with his human head and beaked mouth?

Hua-xu placed her own foot inside the giant's footprint, then quietly went on her way.

No one knows how it happened, but a little while later she gave birth to a child, who was just as extraordinary as the giant's footprint. She named him Fu-xi. His body was half human, half snake, and he had the head of a man, the teeth of a turtle, and the lips of a dragon. His white beard was so long that it fell down as low as his snake's tail.

On stone carvings depicting him, Fu-xi is shown holding a square, a symbol of masculinity.

BROTHER AND SISTER

Fu-xi lived on earth, but climbed into the heavens whenever he wanted using an immense tree as a stairway: its roots went deep into the ground and its crown touched the sky.

Fu-xi knew everything about religion and magic. With his keen eye, he carefully observed how the spider spun her web. Using her model, he invented nets for hunting and fishing. But there was no one to benefit from his teaching, for human beings did not yet exist.

Fu-xi had a sister named Nu-wa. Like him, she had a human head and a snake's tail, but not all the time! She had the power to transform whenever she wanted, but never more than seventy times a day. Nu-wa is depicted holding a compass, symbol of the circle and of femininity. It was

she who first thought of peopling the earth.

HOW THE FIRST PEOPLE WERE CREATED

One day, Nu-wa took a bit of yellow clay from a pond and began to knead it with great skill. She shaped creatures never before seen: men and women just like us, with round heads and rectangular feet.

After she had made a good number, she decided to dip a rope into a pool of mud and then swing it around in the air, flinging drops in all directions. Every drop that fell to the ground turned into a man or a woman. Soon, there was a multitude.

It is said that those who were created from clay became the wealthy nobility, while the others, barely formed and made from mud, became the poor and the weak. But for the moment, none of these new creatures knew how to do anything, not even the children. Nu-wa would have to teach them.

THE WORK OF SOVEREIGNS

Fu-xi was sitting on the square summit of a hill. The breath of the eight winds, coming from the eight directions—east, northeast, north, northwest, west, southwest, south, and southeast—inspired him to form the eight trigrams that are the basis of the earliest Chinese writing.

Thus, Fu-xi taught humankind not only how to hunt and fish, but also how to begin to write.

One day, catching sight of a phoenix, Fu-xi fell

THE TRIGRAMS OF FU-XI

THE EIGHT TRIGRAMS, SO CALLED
BECAUSE THEY CONSIST OF THREE
PARTS, STAND FOR THE FORCES OF
NATURE: EARTH, SKY, WATER, FIRE,
MOUNTAIN, THUNDER, WIND, AND THE
MIST THAT RISES FROM THE LAKES.

into deep thought while observing it.

The phoenix is a magnificent legendary bird. Enormous in size, it is part peacock, part pheasant, and part rooster. It is so delicate it eats only bamboo seeds. While watching it, Fu-xi noted that it alighted only on plane trees, but not on any others. This gave him the idea to chop the trunk of a particularly tall plane tree into three pieces and then to knock on each piece. The piece that had touched the earth sounded too deep and low; the piece that had thrust up into the sky was too sharp; but the piece from the middle, the one people used to rest their backs against, rang with a sound that was just right— not too high, not too low. So Fu-xi carved that piece, making a zither from the wood. Similarly, Nu-wa invented the flute. With these, humans could play music in honor of the gods.

Fu-xi and Nu-wa devoted themselves to the work of civilizing humankind. In stories they are called "The Sovereigns" or "The August Ones." Their kindly and generous reign lasted one hundred and twenty years.

GONG-GONG'S REBELLION

At this time a water god named Gong-gong, who was also a monstrous demon, decided to rebel. Was he angry that he could not be master of the earth, or did he rise up to take revenge against the god of fire? Anything is possible, but whatever the reason, Gong-gong was a force with which to reckon. His power was terrifying. He had the face of a man, but his eyes never moved. His hair was red and he had the body of a dragon. He never got hungry or thirsty. With all his force, he butted his head against Mount Bu Zhou—a mountain in the northwest and one of the four mountains on earth that served as the pillars of heaven and held up the sky. The collision was so violent that the sky in that region shattered like glass, leaving a wide hole in the

firmament. To keep from falling into emptiness, the stars slipped off to the northwest. The blow also shook the earth, causing it to tilt to the southeast. This cosmic disturbance caused floods and fires. At any moment unimaginable catastrophes could come from the broken sky: fiery rain, monsters, or worse!

STONES AND POWDER

Nu-wa wanted to protect humankind, her own

creatures. To repair the shattered sky, she smelted together stones of five colors, but could not fit them together well enough. She therefore sacrificed a large turtle and used its legs to replace the pillar and prop up the sky. Then she made a powder of reeds to patch up the hole. Although she saved the world from destruction, she was not completely successful in her repairs: the hole in the sky was not perfectly patched and the earth remained at a tilt. This is why the waters of all the rivers and streams in China flow eastward, pouring their waters into the great ocean that formed there in a vast, hollow basin. Because of the earth's new tilt seasons appeared, and rivers brought more water onto the land. As a result, the trees, flowers and crops grew green, bloomed

and turned golden, each trying to outdo the other.

Some say that from then on the sun did not dare go to where Nu-wa had patched up the sky, and so a kindly dragon set himself up there with a torch in his mouth. He could not keep light from illuminating the emptiness behind him, but in the end he was able to shine some light in what would have remained a black hole.

POWERFUL LITTLE PEAS

As for Gong-gong, he was finally defeated by the god of fire. Gong-gong's son and ally, a demon every bit as wild as he, was also killed in the battle, and then reborn in the shape of a terrifying ghost. But as luck would have it, anyone who feared him had a perfect weapon against him. The ghost had one weakness: he trembled with fear before a plate of red peas! All one had to do was to eat them on the day of the winter solstice to be protected from his terrible blows for a whole year.

THE THIRD SOVEREIGN

Like Fu-xi and Nu-wa, Shen-nong also was born of a goddess. One day as Shen-nong's mother was out walking, she failed to notice a dragon that appeared from the clouds and knocked her on the head. Perhaps this is why Shen-nong's own head—with the nose, ears and horns of an ox—is not the kind you normally see on a human body, which is what this god had. Honored as a god of

medicine, health and agriculture, Shen-nong is the one who understood how to bring forth the six grains that would spread to all countries of the world, from wheat in the north to rice in the south. He invented the plow and developed the art of using it. He also taught humans about arithmetic and trade, and more about how to write. He even showed them how to use fire for making sacrifices to the gods.

DEVOTED TO THE END

Shen-nong's highest knowledge, however, was in how to use plants to cure illness. With his whip, he lashed flowers, fruits, leaves and roots to make their powers spring forth from them.

He used them on himself and drew conclusions, such as: dried sugared pears are good for coughs, and the hawthorn plant gives one a good appetite.

Shen-nong never stopped increasing his knowledge. He swallowed up to seventy plants a day just to learn their secrets. In the end, from sheer devotion to experimentation, he died of poisoning. By then he had reigned for one hundred and twenty years.

SQUARE EARTH, ROUND SKY

FOR THE EARLIEST CHINESE, THE EARTH WAS SQUARE. ABOVE IT, THE SKY WAS ROUND AND FORMED A DOME.

ON EARTH THERE WAS AN EMPIRE WITH FIVE DIRECTIONS, ONE FOR EACH CARDINAL POINT: EAST, WEST, NORTH, SOUTH AND BELOW THE SUN AT ITS ZENITH, THE MIDDLE.

FOUR MOUNTAINS HELD UP THE SKY LIKE PILLARS, AND EACH OF THE FOUR SOVEREIGNS OF THE CARDINAL POINTS HAD A PALACE ON HIS OWN MOUNTAIN. THEY RULED OVER THE GODS OF NATURE, THE WIND, AND THE WATERS, AS WELL AS THE MYTHOLOGICAL ANIMALS. ALL FOUR SOVEREIGNS, IN THEIR TURN, WERE SUBJECTS OF THE MOST POWERFUL OF ALL, THE EMPEROR OF THE MIDDLE, WHO WAS ALSO CALLED THE YELLOW EMPEROR OR THE CELESTIAL EMPEROR.

BEYOND THE FOUR CORNERS OF THE
EMPIRE, WERE EXPANSES OF
UNKNOWN LANDS WHERE OTHER
PEOPLES, STRANGERS AND BARBAR-
IANS, LIVED. PAST THESE LANDS THE
FOUR OCEANS BEGAN, AFTER WHICH
THERE CAME UNENDING EMPTINESS. IT
WAS THERE, WITHOUT A DOUBT, THAT
DEMONS HAD THEIR KINGDOMS.
NOTHING GOOD COULD COME FROM
THERE.

2

STORIES OF PAN-GU

There are two other creation stories that came later than those about the Three Sovereigns. They are very well known in China and, as you will see, they share the same hero, Pan-gu, but in different guises.

THE EGG OF THE WORLD

At the beginning of the world, heaven and earth were mixed together. They formed an egg made of one and the same substance, and in the middle of this egg was Pan-gu.
He grew in this egg for over eighteen thousand years. At the end of this time, Pan-gu looked a lot like a giant—a giant who was already very, very big. When he suddenly awoke, he cracked his home—the egg of heaven and earth—in two, with one swing of his axe.

Pan-gu's great axe blow separated the heavens, which rose up, from the earth, which spread out below.

OF FLEAS AND HUMANS

With heaven up above, earth down below and Pan-gu in the middle, all three continued to grow for another eighteen thousand years. The heavens rose higher and higher, the earth sank lower and lower and Pan-gu, who filled the space in between, grew bigger and bigger.

When heaven and earth had reached their perfect sizes, they stopped growing and became fixed into place. Then Pan-gu died and all the parts of his body transformed themselves: his

chest, his stomach, his arms and his legs turned into mountains. His two eyes took their place in the sky: his left eye became the sun and his right eye the moon. His breath became one with the clouds and the wind. His voice turned into thunder. His blood formed rivers. The hair on his body became trees, and his whiskers, stars. One version

YIN AND YANG

IN CHINESE THOUGHT, THE ELEMENTS OF NATURE ARE OFTEN INTERPRETED AS BEING EITHER YIN OR YANG. THE HOT AND LIGHT ELEMENT FROM THE EGG OF THE WORLD THAT BECAME THE SKY IS THE MALE ELEMENT, OR YANG.

THE HEAVIER AND COLDER PART OF THE EGG THAT BECAME THE EARTH IS THE FEMALE ELEMENT, OR YIN.

of the story adds that even his fleas transformed into humans. In the same way, the four other kinds of things held to be living—animals, plants, spirits and ghosts—were made.

Thus, all categories of living things belong to the same family, all having been born in the same way. They also are intimately connected to nature and to the cosmos, since everything was once Pan-gu.

A DOG FOR AN ANCESTOR

For the Yao, the Chinese from the south, humans were born from Pan-gu, but in a different way. For them, Pan-gu was a dog—a very unusual dog, whose name in that region was Pan-hu. To begin with, he sprang from an insect still in its cocoon. Yes, a cocoon! Where did this cocoon come from? From the ear of a lady of the palace in the Celestial Empire.

For three years the lady had wondered what could possibly be giving her such an earache. Well, it was this cocoon that turned into a dog the moment it appeared! Not just into any dog, mind you, but a dog of five different colors!

This extraordinary dog, who could only have the Celestial Emperor as his master, was named Pan-hu and lived at court.

Pan-hu, born from an ear, pricked up his own ears whenever he heard the Celestial Emperor get angry. A group of rebels sought to take his throne from him. Enraged by this, the emperor shouted, "Whoever brings me the head of the rebel leader will receive my youngest daughter as a reward, a mountain of gold and his own city to rule."

With this declaration, the deed was done. The head of General Wu, his enemy, was at the palace. But brought by whom?

By Pan-hu.

He had gone to the rebel camp. No one was suspicious of a dog. He had sidled into camp, gone up to General Wu, and jumped on him, attacking with tooth and claw. When it was over, General Wu had lost his head!

The Celestial Emperor was extremely pleased: his enemy was dead and he was certain of keeping his daughter, his mountain of gold and his city, since a dog cannot marry a woman or be a ruler.

"Oh, yes he can," said the youngest daughter. "A promise is a promise."

She insisted on having Pan-hu as her husband, dog or no dog. With a heavy heart, the emperor accepted his daughter's decision, but only on the condition that the newlyweds would leave not only the palace but the country as well. The wedding was held at court, following which Pan-hu put his young wife onto his colorful back. Some say they went to live on an island, while others mention the grottos of Hunan. Their children are the ancestors of people who still love to dress in bright colors, no doubt in memory of the multicolored dog who married the princess.

PAN-HU'S BELL

Here is yet another version of the story with a different ending.
When the Celestial Emperor realized that the one who had defeated Wu was a dog, he was

delighted. He could not imagine that he would have to keep his promise—impossible! For who would give a daughter away to a dog?

Full of sorrow, Pan-hu understood his situation. The look on a sad dog's face is something everyone can understand. Noticing this, the emperor asked him what the trouble was, and at that moment Pan-hu started to speak! He said that if it bothered the emperor to see his daughter marry a dog, then he could easily turn himself into a man. To do that, all he needed was to spend seven days inside a golden bell.

Obviously (although he didn't say so), no one was allowed to see him during those seven days. Five days passed, but on the sixth, the princess was so curious that she could no longer resist. She looked under the bell. Pan-hu was almost a man: his legs, arms and body had become human, but his head had not. The spell was broken and his transformation could not be completed. Pan-hu would keep his dog's head. The wedding took place in a secret land, and his three sons and one daughter, born without dog heads, were the first human beings.

3

THE FIRST
OF THE FIVE EMPERORS

After the Three Sovereigns—Fu-xi, Nu-wa and Shen-nong—five divinities, all called emperor, would rule successively. These should not be confused with the actual emperors of China, the historical figures who unified and governed the country, even though these were only too happy to be identified with the mythological emperors. Indeed, to ensure their own earthly power, the emperors of China decreed the gods to be their ancestors. To make this seem true, they had chronicles written during their reigns in which the gods bear the title of emperor. This title passed from one mythological emperor to the next, right down to each historical ruler, which is how the emperors of China proved that they were divinely descended.

THE YELLOW EMPEROR

Among the Five Legendary Emperors, Huang Di, the Emperor of the Middle, was the first. He also was called the Yellow Emperor, a name derived from the color of the soil.

Huang Di was the younger half-brother of Shennong, on account of which he succeeded Shennong to the throne. It is told that his mother was standing on a hill when a rainbow or a cloud banded by lightning appeared just as there was a boom of thunder. From this, Huang Di was conceived. In some stories he is portrayed as having the face of a highly intelligent dragon.

AN INVENTOR

During his reign, Huang Di invented a great many things, from the art of war to ball games. At the same time, he gave his people a life altering invention—the creation of cooked food.

THE EMPERORS OF THE SOUTH, EAST, WEST AND NORTH

THE EMPERORS OF THE FOUR CARDINAL POINTS WHO SERVED THE EMPEROR OF THE MIDDLE DIVIDED THE SEASONS, THE FORCES OF NATURE, AND THE COLORS BETWEEN THEM. EACH ALSO HAD HIS OWN ANIMAL.

THE EMPEROR OF THE SOUTH REIGNED OVER SUMMER, FIRE AND RED. HIS ANIMAL WAS THE PHOENIX.

THE EMPEROR OF THE EAST WAS LORD OF SPRING, WOOD AND BLUE. A BLUE DRAGON WAS HIS EMBLEM.

THE EMPEROR OF THE WEST'S SHARE WAS AUTUMN, GOLD AND WHITE. A MAGNIFICENT WHITE TIGER PROTECTED HIM.

THE EMPEROR OF THE NORTH RULED OVER WINTER, WATER AND BLACK. A CREATURE THAT WAS HALF-SNAKE AND HALF-TURTLE ACCOMPANIED HIM.

Though his predecessor, Shen-nong, knew how to sow and grow crops, no one had yet had the idea to cook them before eating them. To be clear, people at that time already had enjoyed the taste of meat, fish, and savory shellfish, but raw. And raw meat, fish and shellfish, no matter how delicious, do not stay fresh for very long. Many people had gotten stomachaches, colic and worse before Huang Di discovered how to roast, boil, broil, fry, sauté and fricassee meat and vegetables.

HUANG DI VERSUS CHI-YOU

But Huang Di's crowning glory was the taming of a number of animals: bears, lynx, tigers, wolves, leopards and eagles. His aim was not to put them in cages, but to enlist them into his army as soldiers.

In other words, Huang Di had enemies, though not many. First he fought Yan Di, the god of fire, said to be his brother, or perhaps the Emperor of the South, and defeated him.

Then Chi-you rose up against him.

Chi-you was one of Huang Di's ministers and owed obedience to him. As his wings suggest, Chi-you was a god of the wind, who also was held to be a god of war. He had a heavy bronze head, pointed horns, hairy ears, six hands, and six feet with water buffalo hooves. He was skillful and intelligent. He understood the art of casting metals and used his knowledge to invent weapons such as lances, sabers, and all kinds of swords.

COMING TO THE AID OF YAN DI

The fight began when Chi-you picked a quarrel with Yan Di right after Yan Di's defeat by Huang Di. Chi-you was so menacing that Yan Di fled, but Chi-you pursued him and recruited men from the south of the country to be his soldiers. Despairing, Yan Di asked Huang Di, to help him. Huang Di was furious that one of his ministers

33

not only had rebelled, but also had involved humans in the private affairs of the gods. With his advance guard of leopards, tigers and bears, he threw himself into battle.

WEAPONS AND MAGIC

Chi-you, lord of the wind, conjured a dense, cottony fog that suddenly enveloped Huang Di's entire army. Disoriented, the soldiers circled around blindly, drawing Chi-you to them by their cries and also massacring each other. Hunag Di needed to save them. He scratched his handsome dragon's head and came up with an idea. He summoned his minister, the prince of winds, who was stronger than Chi-you.

"Get us out of this horror," ordered Huang Di. The prince of winds immediately perfected a magnificent weathervane in the form of a statue standing in a chariot that worked in fog, mist and all other kinds of weather. This amazing invention, a complex geared mechanism, worked by spinning around and then stopping in one direction. That of the wind? No! Of the north? Not exactly! It pointed the way out, just as Huang Di had asked!

Chi-you tried to use magic to shift the fog here and there each time the statue turned, so that he could escape, but he tried in vain. The Celestial Emperor and his army easily found their way out.

Furious, Chi-you stomped the ground with his

buffalo hooves. Far stronger than fog, a storm broke out that engulfed Huang Di.

THE EMPEROR'S DAUGHTER

Fortunately, the emperor had a daughter, Ba, who had the power to bring on drying winds and droughts. Huang Di sent her, with her always burning body, down from heaven. Bald and old as she was, she blew and blew until she was completely worn out, but at last the waters dried up. The unhappy Ba did not have enough energy to climb back up to heaven, so she stayed on earth, where her very presence drove all moisture away. Not a drop could survive near her, so wherever she was the ground cracked and became a desert. Huang Di ordered Ba to go north, which she did, and she has remained on earth ever since. She comes and goes, sometimes lingering too long in the south, and wherever she goes there is drought. To drive the feared and despised Ba away, humans perform rituals and recite incantations.

CHI-YOU'S PUNISHMENT

Chi-you, always the rebel, made a new alliance with the giants, but the Yellow Emperor was stronger than they. Chi-you was taken prisoner, and his fate was sealed: he was condemned to death. The execution was swift: his head was cut off before he could remove his armor. (Some say Chi-you's chains became maple trees, the leaves of which—slightly red from having absorbed drops of his blood—remember him to this day.)

In any case, it actually was his head that was sliced and not his neck for his armor covered him up to his teeth. Thus, the fatal blow struck him above his armor, at ear level, but where our ears are not his, since his were more like the horns on top of his head. This helps to explain the famous "mask of Tao-tie," the face with no chin or body that is often found engraved on vases, cauldrons, and shields in order to display the absolute power of Huang Di, the Emperor of the Middle. Clearly these images were used to scare away spirits or whomever else wanted to rebel like Chi-you.

THE NEW REGULATIONS

Huang Di had not forgotten how Chi-you had enlisted humans into battle. That could not happen again. So he ruled that the gods would

not be allowed to descend to earth without his permission. With his assent, they would travel by dragon only. Believing strongly in order, Huang Di further decreed that the only other role dragons would have would be to make it rain, which meant that henceforth they would live in oceans, rivers and clouds. Such regulations mark the beginning of the Celestial Empire, a strictly ordered period with a multitude of rules. Under Huang Di, what might be called a celestial bureaucracy had begun.

THE GODS OF THE DOORS

And so it was that Huang Di came to oversee the work of his two brothers, two guardian deities named Shen-tu and Yu-lu, whom he charged with watching the ghosts and demons who wander

through the night, and who now were required to report at the gate atop Mount Du Shuo each morning. Each spirit was closely questioned. If it turned out that during the night he had done some evil, he would be tied with a rope made of reeds to the trunk of an astonishing peach tree. And there, without hope of escape, the spirit would be devoured by tigers.

People in antiquity loved this story and put pictures of the two brothers on their entry doors, along with pictures of tigers, to scare away bad spirits. In this way, the brothers came to be known as the gods of the doors. On the day of the winter solstice, a holiday, peach wood and a reed broom were once placed by the door. It was believed that such a broom could sweep away demons, as well as all of the worries that trouble the mind and take the fun out of life.

4

YU THE GREAT

After Huang Di, other emperors ruled over the human world. Each taught humanity secrets born of the heavens. The fourth after Huang Di was named Yao.

Yao's father was a red dragon. His mother was pregnant with him for fourteen months. By the time he was twenty, he was known throughout the country for his wisdom. Thus Huang Di chose him as his successor.

THE GREAT FLOOD

Suddenly a flood, as powerful as it was inexplicable, deluged the world, and the difference between land and sea was lost. All of earth's creations were confused. Enormous waves surged and struck the earth as if trying to sink it. The people who survived this colossal flood took refuge on mountain tops or floating islets, but they remained in great danger. Not only was it unclear where the land ended and the waters began, but the only creatures to rise up from the waves were enormous black snakes and dragons. Would they remain the sole masters of a watery

world? Who could return order from such chaos?

GUN'S PLAN

Faced with this deluge, Emperor Yao ordered Gun, one of his ministers and a deep thinking man, to find a way to stop the flooding. From the start, Gun understood that failure was not a possibility, for at the time people thought nothing of striking each other, cutting off heads, or slicing bodies in half.

So Gun devised a plan to erect huge sea walls to hold back the waters. But the river swelled and rose up against those walls, finally overrunning them and pouring onto the shores. The flood-waters destroyed everything in their path. Instead of solving the problem, Gun had made things worse.

Found guilty, he was condemned to death and killed. His dead body fell to the ground, there to remain. Three years passed.

YU'S PLAN

Meanwhile, Shun, Yao's relative, succeeded him as emperor. Emperor Shun sent a messenger to Gun's body, still intact and exactly where it had fallen. With one blow of his axe, the messenger sliced Gun's body in two.

A horned dragon sprang out of the body and transformed into a man. It was Yu, believed to be Gun's son. He put himself at Shun's service, and agreed to try to stop the floods.

Yu had learned from his father's errors. Since

DRAGONS

CHINESE DRAGONS ARE KIND AND
HELPFUL AS LONG AS THEIR ANGER
ISN'T ROUSED. PEOPLE CALL ON THEM
TO MAKE IT RAIN, BUT THEY ALSO CAN
MAKE IT THUNDER. IN THE SPRING,
THEY FLY UP FROM THE WATERS
TOWARD THE SKY RIDING ON THE
CLOUDS. THEY CAN TAKE UP TO NINE
DIFFERENT FORMS. SOME HAVE SCALES
AND OTHERS HAVE WINGS OR HORNS.
THERE IS NO WAY TO MISS THE
DRAGON THAT REPRESENTS THE
EMPEROR: IT IS THE ONLY ONE WITH
FIVE TALONS ON EACH FOOT.

Gun had not succeeded by raising sea walls, he would dig to lower the riverbed. He also would cut through mountains, create new waterways and divert floodwaters into the sea.

In all probability Yu would never have succeeded without his trusted helper, Ying-long, a river dragon who could dive fearlessly into whirling waters. Yu followed the coast on his tireless horse, who could travel nine thousand miles a day. He dismounted only when Ying-long had indicated with his tail where to dig. Having reached the right place, Yu went to work.

YU'S SUCCESS

Yu's efforts were crowned with success. The waters receded, the river grew calm, and its god, named He Bo, appeared. Then a giant snake led Yu to a cave where Fu-xi himself waited. Fu-xi gave Yu a magical square plate of jade that could measure earth and sky.

Yu continued his work. The waters were now contained by canals, but the ground had still to be won.

THE STRENGTH OF A BEAR

Yu assumed the shape of a bear to split a mountain in two and create the first overland crossing, the Dragon's Pass. The next mountain he broke in three. By clearing away rocks and boulders, he opened the way for the Three Gates Pass. He went from one chasm to the next, unhindered by the unfamiliar dragons whom he often had to finish off. It took him thirteen years of exhausting work to complete his task. Meanwhile, in his human form, he had married, but without revealing that he transformed into a bear to work. As his wife wanted to follow him into the mountains, they agreed that she would wait for his signal, the beating of a drum, before coming to him with his lunch. Once she had left him, he would return to work as a bear.

YU'S CHILD

One day a rock fell, causing Yu's drum to reverberate through the mountains. His wife took this to be his signal and hurried to meet him. Having no idea that she was coming, Yu was still in bear form. As she had never seen him that way, she took fright. Despite Yu's shouts, she ran away. As she ran, she transformed herself into a rock. Yu followed and struck the rock, his wife. It cracked open, and their baby sprang forth. Yu's wife was gone, but he had a son, whom he named Qi and carried away with him.

YU BECOMES EMPEROR

Emperor Shun had grown old. To reward Yu, he named him as his successor. Emperor Yu, however, was also quite tired, for his titanic labors had made his limbs stiff and paralyzed some of his muscles. Indeed he hopped more than walked. Yet, he knew every inch of the country, and he drew up maps for nine provinces. He listed the names of the monsters living in each so everyone could be on guard against them. He had minerals brought from all over the kingdom to cast nine three-legged, bronze cauldrons, upon each of which a map was engraved.

CAULDRONS AND GREED

Heavy and magnificent, the cauldrons were placed at the gates of the palace. They roused the envy of a neighboring ruler who made the following argument: "Since the cauldrons are part of the imperial treasure, anyone who owns them has the right to be emperor. So let us go and seize them." Yu, who heard and saw everything, learned of this plan and sent this message to the covetous king: "The right to rule is given because of a person's abilities as a ruler and not because a person has one or two or even nine cauldrons." The neighbor understood the lesson and thought better of seizing the cauldrons.

Much later an emperor who had succeeded Qi's successors wanted to move the cauldrons to his new residence. To prevent this, a magic force gathered eight of the cauldrons up into the air, where they disappeared. The ninth plunged to the bottom of the river.

Even later still, Qin Shi Huang Di, the first emperor of the Qin dynasty, wishing to clear his mind of the matter, gave an unconditional order: one thousand soldiers must scour the bottom of the river. To protect the cauldron, a dragon emerged from the water and broke the rope holding it, scaring all treasure hunters away forever. Thus the ninth imperial cauldron, hidden in the waters that Yu had tamed, kept its secret.

5

THE CHINESE PARADISES

A PARADISE FOR THE GODS

The paradise of the Chinese gods is where the Queen Mother of the West, Xi Wang Mu, lives. It is almost inaccessible, lying just below the North Star.

North of Mount Kun Lun, the Queen's palace is a jade mountain that touches the earth at its foot and the heavens at its peak.

Guarded by a forest of fires, magical animals, ramparts of gold, and shifting sands, the exquisite hanging gardens around the Queen's palace protected her well.

According to legend, she had two very different guises. In one she had a female face, long flowing hair, the teeth of a tiger, and the tail of a leopard. In this guise she lived in a cave attended by strange green birds with three legs. In her other guise, she appeared as a pretty young woman, and she lived in an elegant palace surrounded by gracious servants. There she held parties and games near a shimmering lake, the smallest pebble of which was considered a precious stone.

Of the seven kinds of precious stones, jade was the most highly prized.

PEACHES AND THE PEACH TREES OF LIFE

Time has no meaning where the peach tree of life grows. Whosoever tastes one of its fruits becomes immortal. The peaches themselves take six thousand years to ripen. First, the peach tree needs to put forth leaves and flowers (every three thousand years), and then its fruit has to ripen (another three thousand years). The day the peaches of life are ripe is called the Queen Mother of the West's birthday. To celebrate, the immortals are invited to a gala feast where they are served bear claws, dragon livers and other rarities before being offered the peaches of life.

On occasion, a human would attend the party as a reward for extraordinary feats. Having bitten into the delicious peach of life, this mortal would return to the paradise of the gods after death to live, feast, and play forever. Thus it happened that a mortal became immortal.

A PARADISE FOR HUMANS

As for the humans who become wise or holy enough to earn eternal life, after death they went to a paradise as well. In Chinese art, these humans are depicted as translucent beings with feathered wings.

In their paradise, they would live a dream life on mountainous islands, in an actual sea, the Sea of the East. They passed their days in white palaces, surrounded by white animals. When it rained, it rained flowers. Even the grass itself was a treasure, used to concoct the elixir of immortality. For that reason alone, emperors sent out their fleets in search of these islands. Being magical, however,

these islands would disappear from view the moment a boat came close to sighting them.

PEARLS, GOLD AND JADE

The wise men in paradise never worried about these things. Every morning they went visiting from island to island, and every evening they went directly home. In their gardens, which grew over seven terraces, there were trees full of pearls and fruits made of jade – a food of the immortals. Tree boughs made sweet music as they swayed in the wind, and blooming lotuses adorned ponds encircled by precious stones. As for the ponds, they were filled with crystal clear water and lined with gold dust. This probably had to do with the fact that beyond all of their privileges, those who were immortal knew the secret of making gold.

Yet even on these blessed islands, all was not perfect.

DRIFTING ISLANDS

In the beginning of the world, five islands floated in the East Sea like graceful barks that would vanish as soon as a ship appeared, which happened from time to time. Rarely, but occasionally, the islands would run up against the shores having allowed themselves to be rocked by the current. This worried some of the island dwellers, who decided to complain to the Celestial Emperor.

He considered their complaint and gave the following orders to a god of the sea winds, Yu-qiang.

First, round up fifteen enormous tortoises. Next, place three tortoises to guard each of the five islands. Third, place one tortoise under each island to support it while putting the other two tortoises on either side to secure it. Fourth, switch the tortoises every sixty thousand years.

This plan was carried out perfectly up to the third order.

THE GIANT FROM THE KINGDOM OF THE COUNT OF DRAGONS

However, even before the second round of tortoises was needed, a giant from the Kingdom of the Count of Dragons came to fish in the East Sea. The count, who ruled over the giant, wanted tortoises so he could burn their shells and read the future from them. In just a few strides, the giant spotted six of the tortoises that had to serve for sixty thousand years. Without hesitating, he dislodged them from under their

JADE

JADE IS A HARD STONE.

ITS COLOR CAN RANGE FROM WHITE TO GREEN, INCLUDING BEIGE, BROWN AND GRAY. IN ANCIENT CHINA, IT WAS SCULPTED AND POLISHED WITH AS MUCH CARE AS PRECIOUS JEWELS. RELIGIOUS OBJECTS MADE OF JADE WERE HIGHLY PRIZED.

PLATES HAVE BEEN FOUND ON WHICH THE CHARACTER FOR BI, MEANING TREASURE, HAS BEEN ENGRAVED.

AS A HIGHLY PRIZED TREASURE, JADE ALSO IS USED AS A LUCKY CHARM.

two islands, piled them up on his huge back, and returned to his country.

DEVASTATION

The two islands, Dai Yu and Yuan Jiao, that had lost their anchors drifted northward, where storms raged. Extraordinarily high waves immediately submerged the islands. Their beautiful palaces and trees, along with everything else, were swallowed up. The immortals, being immortal, did not drown, but found themselves in very unpleasant circumstances, lost on the high seas.

THE EMPEROR'S FURY

Seized with fury, the Celestial Emperor condemned the Kingdom of the Count of Dragons to shrink, along with its giants, who could no longer remain such a dangerous and absurd size. The emperor also made sure that the tortoises belonging to the three remaining islands—Peng Lai, Fang Zhang and Ying Zhou—were in good shape. Since they were, it was decided that they would remain is place for all eternity, guaranteeing refuge to all immortals.

6

THE TEN SUNS
AND THE MOON

In this story, Xi-he is one of the wives of the Celestial Emperor, Jun Di. Together they had ten extraordinary children, who – being suns!—were the only boys of their kind. Every morning, one of them crossed the Valley of Light to the farthest eastern part of the world, bringing dawn to the earth.

THE YOUNG SUNS

Each day the ten suns were brought by their mother to the valley lake where she bathed them near a magnificent tree—a many-branched mulberry tree called Fu Sang in Chinese. After their bath, the ten little suns would climb into the tree, where nine remained in its lower branches. The tenth climbed right up to the top, and from there he jumped into a waiting chariot. This majestic chariot was drawn by shimmering dragons and driven by the suns' mother herself. Carrying the one sun, the dragons soared away. The trip would take an entire day. The chariot crossed the sky until it reached the peak of the

western most mountain, near a tree with red flowers that was so tall it reached the heavens. There the chariot came to a stop, and the dragons, now free, went to frolic in the clouds. As for the little sun, he climbed along the branches of a tree whose flowers were stars radiating light into the falling night.

How did the sun and his mother return to the east? No one knows for sure, but the next morning, there they would be for another new day.

A BAD IDEA

One morning, as a joke, the ten suns all climbed into the chariot. After only the first hour of the day, the heat on earth was suffocating.

Furious, Emperor Jun Di sent Yi, his divine archer, to reestablish order and bring nine suns back down to earth.

Yi already was a hero. He had proven himself worthy of Emperor Jun Di's respect when he had

ARCHERY

IN ANCIENT CHINA, ARCHERY WAS
HIGHLY RESPECTED.

THE EDUCATION OF PRINCES AND
YOUNG NOBLES INVOLVED SIX MAJOR
DISCIPLINES: KNOWLEDGE, RELIGIOUS
RITES, MUSIC, WRITING, DIVINATION,
CHARIOT DRIVING AND ARCHERY.

EVEN THE EMPEROR HIMSELF TOOK
PART IN SACRIFICES TO THE GODS BY
SHOOTING AN ARROW AT THE
SACRIFICIAL ANIMAL.

stopped some flooding by discovering that the Count of the river, an ungainly spirit with the head of a man and the body of a fish, was responsible. When Yi found this river spirit, he did not hesitate to yell at him, even to insult him, before shooting him with his invincible arrows.

The Count was accompanied by his young sister, Chang-e, a beautiful young woman. Yi saw her, though not all that clearly. Just well enough to graze her hair with his arrow. She took this to be a declaration of love and agreed to become his wife.

YI'S SOLUTION

Yi quickly got under the blazing chariot of the ten suns. He didn't waste time by giving them any warning. There was only one way to accomplish what he had to do. With his infallible bow, he killed nine of the heedless suns one by one. As each sun fell, a golden raven with three feet flew forth with his spirit.

This sent the emperor into an even greater fury than before. He had not given the order to have his sons killed. To punish the archer Yi, he stripped him of immortality and condemned him to life as a mortal.

Yi was not happy about this given that he had succeeded in bringing order back into the world, and the suns would not be able to repeat their dangerous game as only one of them

remained. In the future, it still could happen that several suns would appear in the sky at the same time, but that would be of the order of a mirage, or an omen announcing a catastrophe or a momentous change, such as the naming of a new emperor.

YI AND THE QUEEN MOTHER OF THE WEST

Determined to get his immortality back, Yi took the path leading to Mount Kun Lun where the magical palace of Xi Wang Mu stood. Won over by Yi's charms, the Queen Mother willingly gave him a small box containing the elixir of immortality. If he took half of what she gave him, he would regain eternal life on earth, but if he took all of it, he would gain entrance to the paradise of the gods.

YI, CHANG-E, AND THE MOON

Yi brought his treasure home and explained everything to his wife, Chang-e. But temptation got the better of her, and when Yi was out, she quickly took all of the elixir. Then, fearing her husband's wrath, she hurried to hide herself as high up and far away as possible, which turned out to be on the moon. This is why the Chinese talk of the woman on the moon, while we refer to the man in the moon.

It is said that Chang-e is still on the moon today, living in the Palace of Solitude, a frozen and lonely place.

It also is told that when she arrived on the moon, she found a rabbit, some say a jade rabbit, that protected her from Yi when he chased after her. The rabbit is now busy for all eternity, making the elixir of life. Sometimes there is a third person with them, an old woman, perhaps the Queen Mother herself, who makes bundles of firewood. She gathers the branches of a mysterious tree that never stops growing. Some think it might have been a cinnamon tree, while others believe it to have been the cassia tree.

THE MOON

THERE IS A CELEBRATION OF THE
MOON EVERY SEPTEMBER.

PEOPLE TAKE WALKS AT NIGHT TO
GAZE AT THE MOON, SHINING BRIGHT
IN THE SKY OR REFLECTED IN THE
WATER. CHILDREN HAPPILY CARRY
LANTERNS MADE OF COLORED PAPER.
EVERYONE EATS LITTLE SUGARY CAKES
THAT TASTE LIKE WATERMELLON OR
DATES AND ARE CALLED — MOON
CAKES!

SOME PEOPLE DAYDREAM, RECALLING
THE LEGEND OF AN OLD MAN ON THE
MOON WHO MAKES LISTS OF THOSE
WHO WILL MEET AND MARRY DURING
THE COMING YEAR. DAYDREAMING, THEY
WONDER: WHO WILL IT BE?

7

THE HERDER AND THE WEAVER

At the beginning of this story the sky has yet to get all of its stars.

There was a young man, an orphan, who had nowhere to live except with his brother and sister-in-law, neither of whom liked him. He worked hard in the fields, where his only companion was their old ox. He took care of it, fed it, groomed it, and the ox looked at him with its peaceful eyes. From one sad day to the next, life went on. Until one day when the ox opened his mouth and said: "Leave this house, my boy. Ask to bring me along and let us go from here."

The young man's brother was happy to keep the cottage and the fields all for himself, so he let the ox go without a second thought. Good riddance!

THE DAUGHTERS OF THE EMPEROR OF HEAVEN

The ox and the herder walked without stopping until they came to the foot of a mountain. There the young man built a cabin. The ox, who seemed to know what to do, spoke again.

"Down that way there is a hidden lake where the seven daughters of the Emperor of Heaven go to

bathe. Without letting anyone see you, take the clothes of the seventh sister and hide."

The herder listened to the ox and without asking a single question, he did exactly as he was told. Taken aback to find her clothes gone, the daughter of the Emperor of Heaven was seized with dread. Her sisters, worried about disobeying their parents by coming home late, ran off, leaving her all alone.

THE WEAVER

At that moment the young man showed himself and told the girl the sad story of his life.

The girl was so moved that she offered to marry him at once. In no time the weaver, the herder, the ox and the two infants who had rapidly come into the world were happy. The young wife could weave and sew to perfection. When still in her father's palace, she had been the celestial weaver, weaving wondrous clouds of gold and the red fabric of the setting sun. Now that she was a mother, she continued to weave splendid brocades, and sold them to feed her family.

THE QUEEN OF HEAVEN

The ox, who was growing old, spoke to the young man for a third time:

"Do not be sad to see me die, but keep my hide. When you make a wish, place it over your shoulders and your wish will be granted."

Meanwhile, the Queen of Heaven, the weaver's

THE OX

LONG AGO, THE OX LIVED AS A STAR IN THE SKY. ONE DAY, THE CELESTIAL EMPEROR SENT HIM DOWN TO EARTH TO INFORM HUMANKIND OF THIS:

IT HAD BEEN DECIDED THAT THEY SHOULD FARM THE EARTH SUFFICIENTLY TO ALLOW THEM TO EAT ONCE EVERY THREE DAYS.

BUT THE OX MADE A MISTAKE. INSTEAD HE TOLD THE HUMANS THAT THEY HAD TO WORK ENOUGH TO EAT THREE TIMES A DAY. TO MAKE UP FOR THIS TERRIBLE MISTAKE (IT ALREADY WAS ALMOST IMPOSSIBLE TO PRODUCE ENOUGH FOOD TO EAT ONCE A DAY), THE EMPEROR ORDERED THE OX TO REMAIN ON EARTH TO HELP HUMANS GROW ENOUGH TO HAVE THAT MUCH TO EAT! THIS IS WHY THE PEACEFUL AND PATIENT OX HAS HELPED WITH THE WORK OF THE FIELDS EVER SINCE.

mother, was worried that her seventh daughter had not come home from the lake. Time and time again, she looked for her there. Finally, on a day when the herder was away in the fields, the Queen Mother found her daughter. Furious, she snatched her daughter from her home and without further ado she carried her up into the heavens.

THE OX'S HIDE

Inside the cabin, the weaver's children cried miserably. When their father understood what had happened, he placed the ox's hide over his back, laid a wooden yoke across his shoulders, put his two children into two baskets hanging on either side of the yoke, and wished to fly straight to his wife. But the Queen of Heaven perceived his wish. To keep him from reaching her daughter, the Queen took a pin from her hair and scratched

a thick line between them across the sky. It is said that this is how the Milky Way, called the Silver River or the River of Heaven in Chinese, was created.

SEPARATED STARS

The vast expanse between husband and wife was impossible to cross. It is told that in time the herder and the weaver became stars. Their names are Altair and Vega, and they remain to this day. Sadly the herder and the weaver lost each other, but for Altair and Vega there is hope, since once a year they meet again. On that night (the seventh day of the seventh lunar month) all magpies leave the earth, flying into the celestial realm until morning. In the sky, they arrange themselves between the herder and the weaver, forming a downy bridge. The two lovers run across them with their starry feet, which explains why the magpies return to earth with such ruffled-looking wings.

Should you ever see magpies fluttering around during the day on the seventh day of the seventh lunar month, reproach them a thousand times for forgetting their bridge and forcing the lovers to wait another year before spending a night together.

8

THE INVENTION OF SILK

The breeding of silkworms and the making of silk remained a Chinese invention and a secret for hundreds of years. The advent of worm into silk is a story in and of itself.

THE PROMISE

Imagine a young girl. She misses her dear father who has gone on a trip to a faraway land. She is the only one left in the house and her only companion is the horse in the stable. Having no one else to talk to, one day she says to the horse rather dreamily:

"If you could bring me back my father, I do believe that I would marry you!"

To her great surprise, the horse sets off at a gallop. Without hesitating, he goes directly to where her father is.

"My horse!" her father exclaims in astonishment.

Surprised but happy, he mounts his horse. The horse neighs and pulls at its bridle, as if ready to return to where it had just come from.

HORSES

TOWARD THE MID-FIFTH CENTURY BCE, THE CHINESE LEARNED HOW TO RIDE HORSES FROM THE PEOPLE OF THE STEPPES.

THIS, IN TURN, CHANGED HOW PEOPLE IN CHINA DRESSED. TO RIDE, THEY STARTED WEARING PANTS UNDER THEIR ROBES.

AN EMPEROR WOULD RAID A VILLAGE JUST TO SHOW HOW BEAUTIFUL, SWIFT AND ELEGANT HIS HORSES WERE, SO THAT PEOPLE WOULD CALL THEM, THE HORSES OF HEAVEN.

MOREOVER, EMPERORS WERE OFTEN BURIED IN ENORMOUS TOMBS SURROUNDED BY LIFE-SIZE STATUES OF THEIR HORSES AND HORSEMEN. IT IS SAID THAT THE SCULPTED HORSES THAT GUARD THE TEMPLES COME TO LIFE AT NIGHT TO GALLOP UNDER THE SILVERY MOON.

"What is he trying to say?" wonders the father. He lets his horse guide him. As if it has wings, the horse makes the return trip in a single bound.

THE HORSE'S HIDE

Father and daughter are overjoyed to see each other again. As for the horse, he returns to his stable and waits for his reward, which never comes. So he stops eating and stomps and bucks whenever he sees the girl.

Seeing her father perplexed, the girl tells him of the promise she made as a joke.

"Above all, do not breathe a word of this to anyone," her father immediately commands, "and from now on, I forbid you to go outside." Taking his crossbow, he aims his arrow at the head of the lovesick horse, and kills it. He flays and stretches its hide in the courtyard. At that

moment, his foolish daughter comes outside and begins to mock the horse: "Oh, there you are, the horse who wanted to marry me! You're a sorry sight now, you old nag!"

At these words, the horse's hide flies into the air, wrapping itself tightly around the girl, lifting her up and disappearing into the sky.

THE COCOON

The father searches for his daughter day and night. At the end of three days, he finds her. She has turned into a huge cocoon that hangs from the branch of a mulberry tree. When he brings her before the Celestial Emperor's court, she still has the face of a pretty girl, but otherwise she is a worm with silk thread coming out of her mouth. The Celestial Empress takes hold of this thread and unwinds it, intending to weave with it. From her hands comes the very first piece of silk.

Chinese Characters	Names in Pinyin	Pronunciation
魃	Ba	(b + a)
壁	Bi	(b + ee)
不周山	Bu Zhou Shan	(boo) + (zhr + o) + (shan)
嫦娥	Chang-e	(chr + ah + ng) + (uh)
蚩尤	Chi-you	(chr +i) + (y + oh)
岱与	Dai Yu	(dai) + (y+ü)
度朔	Du Shuo	(do) + (shoo + oh)
方丈	Fang Zhang	(f + ang) + (jr + ah + ng)
伏羲	Fu-xi	(foo) + (shi)
扶桑	Fu Sang	(foo) + (sah +ng)
共工	Gong-gong	(g + ong) + (g + ong)
鲧	Gun	(g + oo +n)
河伯	He Bo	(huh) + (b + oh)
后土	Hou-tu	(hou) + (tu)
华胥	Hua-xu	(hoo + wah) +(shü)
黄帝	Huang Di	(hoo + ang) + (dee)
俊帝	Jun Di	(Jün) + (dee)
昆仑山	Kun Lun Shan	(kwoon)+(loo + un)+ (shan)
女娲	Nu-wa	(n + yü) + (g + wah)
盘古	Pan-gu	(p + an) + (goo)
盘瓠	Pan-hu	(p + an) + (hoo)

Chinese Characters	Names in Pinyin	Pronunciation
蓬莱	Peng Lai	(p + hung) + (lie)
启	Qi	(chee)
秦始皇帝	Qin Shi Huang Di	(chin)+ (shr + i)+ (huang)+ (dee)
神农	Shen-nong	(shr + en) + (no + ng)
神荼	Shen-tu	(shr + en) + (to)
舜	Shun	(shoo + en)
饕餮	Tao-tie	(tao) + (ti + eh)
吴	Wu	(woo)
羲和	Xi-he	(shi) + (he)
西王母	Xi Wang Mu	(shi) + (wan) + (moo)
炎帝	Yan Di	(y + ane) + (dee)
尧	Yao (emperor)	(y + ow)
瑶	Yao (tribe)	(y + ow)
羿	Yi	(yee)
瀛洲	Ying Zhou	(ying) + (joe)
員嬌	Yuan Jiao	(you +en)+ (jee + ow)
应龙	Ying-long	(ying) + (long)
禹	Yu	(yü)
郁垒	Yu-lu	(you + lü)
禺强	Yu-qiang	(you) + (chee + i + ang)

Chinese Characters for Some of the Words that Appear in the Myths

天 Sky

地 Earth

水 Water

河 River

星 Star

皇 Emperor

男 Man

女 Woman

孩 Child

日 Sun

月 Moon

龙 Dragon

凤 Phoenix

馬 Horse

牛 Buffalo

龟 Turtle

虎 Tiger

玉 Jade

珠 Pearl

絲 Silk